Karen's School Trip

Natalie

**Look for these
and other books about Karen
in the
Baby-sitters Little Sister series:**

Little Sister

Karen's School Trip

Ann M. Martin

Illustrations by Susan Tang

A
LITTLE APPLE
PAPERBACK

SCHOLASTIC INC.
New York Toronto London Auckland Sydney

ISBN 0-590-44859-5

12 11 10 9 8 7   5 6 7/9

Printed in the U.S.A.   40

First Scholastic printing, January 1992

For Sherry

Karen's School Trip

Natalie

Lions and Tigers and Bears

"Who can tell me the names of some wild animals?" asked Ms. Colman. (Ms. Colman is my second-grade teacher here at Stoneybrook Academy. She is so, so nice.)

Pamela Harding raised her hand. "Elephants," she said.

Bobby Gianelli raised his hand. "Kangaroos," he said.

I raised my hand. "Lions and tigers and bears," I said. "Like in *The Wizard of Oz.*"

I am Karen Brewer. I am seven years old. I am the youngest kid in Ms. Colman's room. But I do not care. I have lots of friends in my class. My two *best* friends are even in my class. (I am gigundoly lucky.) My best friends are Hannie Papadakis and Nancy Dawes. Pamela Harding and Bobby Gianelli are not my best friends. In fact, Pamela is my best enemy. Bobby is okay, I guess. *His* best friend is Ricky Torres, and Ricky is my pretend husband. We got married on the playground one time.

"Very good," said Ms. Colman. "Who knows what a wild animal is?"

"A jungle animal?" suggested Hannie.

I turned around and smiled at her. (Hannie and Nancy get to sit next to each other in the back row. I have to sit in the front row because I wear glasses.)

"A jungle animal *is* wild," agreed Ms. Colman. "But what makes him wild? Why is he wild?"

I heard Bobby whisper, "Because he is a *party* animal, get it?" But I did not laugh, since I love my teacher.

Nobody could answer Ms. Colman's

2

question, so she said, "Is a farm animal wild?"

"No!" cried my friends and I.

"Why not?"

I remembered to raise my hand again. "Because someone feeds it?" I said.

"Terrific!" exclaimed Ms. Colman. "People take care of farm animals. An animal that is cared for by people is called a *domestic* animal. A *wild* animal lives on its own."

In science class, we had been learning about animals. Now we were going to learn about wild animals. That sounded like fun. Ms. Colman began to pass around some worksheets. Before Ricky Torres had even gotten one, he raised his hand.

"Yes, Ricky?" said Ms. Colman.

"I don't feel well," he replied.

I glanced at Ricky. He sits next to me. This is because he wears glasses, too. (*All* glasses-wearers have to sit in the first row. I think that is a rule.) Ricky had been very quiet that day. Usually, I have to poke him and tell him to stop talking. But not on that day. Ricky just sat at his desk, resting his chin on his hand.

I jumped away from him in case he was going to throw up.

"Does your tummy hurt?" asked Ms. Colman. (She must have been afraid of throw up, too.)

Ricky shook his head. "No. I feel hot."

Ms. Colman rested her hand on his forehead. "I think you have a fever," she said.

A fever. Well, that was interesting.

"Karen, would you please walk Ricky to the nurse's office?" asked Ms. Colman.

"Sure!" I cried. "Come on, Ricky." I led him down the hall and into the nurse's office. (The nurse's office always smells funny. So does the nurse, but she is nice.)

Our nurse is named Mrs. Pazden. She let me sit with Ricky while she took his temperature. "One hundred and one!" exclaimed Mrs. Pazden. "I will call your parents. You ought to be home in bed, Ricky. Come lie down on the cot."

" 'Bye, Ricky," I said. "I better go now. I hope you get well soon."

" 'Bye, Karen," replied Ricky. "Thanks."

We are supposed to walk through the hallways at school. But I did not remember that. I ran all the way back to Ms. Colman's room. I burst through the door. "Ricky has one hundred and one!" I announced. "Mrs. Pazden wants him to go home."

"Wow!" cried my classmates. They were as impressed as I was.

2

My Little House

At home that afternoon, I spread around my news about Ricky. When Nancy Dawes's mother dropped me at my house I ran right inside. "Mommy! Andrew!" I yelled.

"Indoor voice, honey," Mommy reminded me. "And we are in the kitchen."

I lowered my voice. "Guess what," I said.

"What?" asked Andrew. (He is my little brother. He is not even five yet.)

"Ricky got sick in school today. He had to go home."

7

"Did he throw up?" asked Andrew.

"No. He got a fever. Mommy, can I call Kristy and tell her?"

"I suppose so," said Mommy.

Kristy is *thirteen* years old. She is my stepsister. She lives in a different house. My family is sort of hard to explain. See, really I have *two* families. This is because my parents are divorced. A long time ago, Mommy and Daddy were married. That was when they had Andrew and me. Then they decided to get a divorce. They did not love each other anymore. Mommy and Daddy loved Andrew and me a lot, but they did not want to live together. So Mommy moved out of our big house. She took Andrew and me with her. We moved into a little house. (Daddy stayed in the big house. He had grown up there. Both of the houses are here in Stoneybrook, Connecticut.)

After awhile, Mommy and Daddy each got married again. Mommy married Seth. He is my stepfather. He lives with us at my little house. He brought along his cat, Rocky, and his dog, Midgie. I have a pet at the little house, too. She is a rat named Emily Junior.

Daddy married Elizabeth. She is my stepmother. She moved into the big house with Daddy. And she brought along her children — all four of them! Three are boys. My stepbrothers. Sam and Charlie are in high school. David Michael is seven, like me. And Kristy is my stepsister. She babysits. She is a very fun sitter. I just love Kristy.

It is a good thing the big house is so big, because *more* people live in it. Daddy and Elizabeth adopted a little girl. She is two and a half. Her name is Emily Michelle. She came from a country called Vietnam. After Emily arrived, Nannie moved in. She is Kristy's grandmother, which means she is my stepgrandmother. She helps take care of Emily, especially when Daddy and Elizabeth are at work. There are some pets at the big house, too. A cat and a dog and two goldfish. Plus, Andrew and I live there every other weekend. (The rest of the time we live at the little house.)

Sometimes I wish Mommy and Daddy were still married. But mostly I think having two families is okay. You know what? Andrew and I have two of so many things that I call us Andrew Two-Two and Karen Two-Two. (I made up those names after Ms. Colman read a book to my class. The book was called *Jacob Two-Two Meets the Hooded Fang*.) We have two houses, two mommies, two daddies, two cats, and two dogs. And I have my two best friends. Hannie lives near Daddy's house. Nancy lives next door to Mommy's house. I also have two stuffed cats. They look just the same. Moosie stays at the big house. Goosie stays at the little house. I even have two pieces of Tickly, my special blanket. Before, I had only one Tickly, but I kept leaving him at one house or the other. I do not like to fall asleep without Tickly. So I cut my blanket in half. Now I have one half at each house.

Of course, I do not have two of *every-thing*. Even so, I just love having two houses. I like to be at the little house because it is peaceful and quiet. I like to be at the big house because it is noisy and exciting and full of people. Big-house weekends are always wonderful. I get to see Kristy and Emily and Nannie. Sometimes when I am at my little house, I miss my big-house family. Mommy says that is okay. She says it shows I love my big-house family.

That is true.

3

A Trip to the Zoo

The next day was Tuesday. Seth drove Nancy and me to school.

"I wonder if Ricky will be back today," I said to Nancy. "If he is not, I should probably make him a get well card. After all, he is my husband."

"One hundred and one is a very big temperature," said Nancy. "I bet Ricky will be absent today."

Nancy was right. Ricky was absent. So was Natalie Springer. (Natalie is another glasses-wearer who sits in the front row.)

"Lucky ducks, lucky ducks," I sang when I saw the empty desks. I just adore school. But every now and then I like to stay at home and lie in bed and read books. When I am sick Mommy brings me tea and toast and extra pillows. I feel gigundoly cozy. (If I am not *too* sick.)

"Class, may I have your attention, please?" said Ms. Colman. She was sitting at her desk. I noticed a piece of Kleenex stuffed up her sleeve. Ms. Colman pulled it out and dabbed at her nose. "I have an announcement to make," she went on. Oh, goody! Ms. Colman's Surprising Announcements are usually very wonderful. "We have been learning about animals for several weeks now. So I thought we would take a field trip," she said.

I leaped out of my seat. "Yea!" I cried.

"Karen," Ms. Colman said patiently, "indoor voice. And please take your seat." Sniff, sniff. (Ms. Colman blew her nose.)

"Sorry," I replied. I sat down again.

"One week from Friday, we will go to the zoo. We will visit the Bedford Zoo. It is an hour away from Stoneybrook. We will travel on a bus."

"Cool! A bus!" exclaimed Bobby.

"A field trip!" cried Leslie Morris.

My classmates were talking away. Nobody raised their hand. Ms. Colman did not get angry. She just blew her nose and waited for us to calm down.

"Gosh," I said to Bobby. "I hope Ricky and Natalie get well. I do not want them to miss the trip. That would be awful."

"My mom says the flu is going around," said Bobby. "I bet Ricky caught it. I bet he gave it to Natalie. She sits right next to him."

"Well, they have a week and a half to get better," I said. "That is a long time."

After lunch, Ms. Colman said, "Class, today we will begin a new project. It will be part of our animal studies." Sniff, sniff.

(A box of Kleenex had appeared on Ms. Colman's desk. She reached into it a lot.)

I raised my hand. "Ms. Colman, do you have the sniffles?"

"I think so," she said.

"You should drink lots of orange juice," I told her. "It is full of vitamin C."

"Thank you, Karen."

"You're welcome. What is our new project?"

"In a few minutes," Ms. Colman said, "I will give each of you a piece of paper. The paper will be folded up. Inside you will find a secret word. That word will be the name of a wild animal. But it will probably be a type of animal you have never heard of. During the next few days, we will go to the library. I want you to find information about your animal. I want you to find pictures, too. Then you will make a clay model of your animal. You will become sculptors. You may paint your models, too."

Oh, boy! Way cool!

Ms. Colman handed around the papers. My secret word was *capybara*. Ms. Colman was right. I had never heard of capybaras. But I wanted to learn about them. I couldn't wait to be a sculptor.

4

Capybaras

"Achoo! Achoo!"

"Bless you," I said.

"Thank you," replied Ms. Colman.

"Do you have a cold now?" I asked her.

"I guess so. But I do not feel too bad."

It was Wednesday. Ricky and Natalie were still absent. They were not the only ones. Ms. Colman took attendance. Two more kids did not raise their hands and say, "Here!" when she called their names. They were Pamela Harding and Bobby Gianelli.

Wow. Four people with the flu, I

thought. I wondered how long the flu lasts. What if a lot more kids got sick, and on the day of our school trip hardly anybody was in school? Would we still get to go to the zoo?

I decided I better ask Ms. Colman.

I raised my hand.

"Yes?" said my teacher.

"What if a whole lot of kids have the flu next Friday? What if most of the class is absent on the day of our trip?"

"Most of the class?" repeated Ms. Colman. "I suppose we would cancel the trip. We would go some other time."

"Oh."

I guess I looked very sad because Ms. Colman said, "We really would go later. I promise. We would probably go in the spring."

Ms. Colman did not understand. I wanted to go to the zoo on Friday. I could not wait until the spring. I am not very good at waiting.

"Achoo!" Ms. Colman sneezed again.

But she didn't sneeze into a Kleenex like she did yesterday. She sneezed into a very beautiful pink handkerchief. (I can only sneeze into Kleenexes. Mommy and Seth do not like to wash dirty handkerchiefs. Even Seth does not have a handkerchief.)

"Bless you," I said again.

"Thank you," Ms. Colman said again.

After lunch, Ms. Colman took my class-mates and me to the school library. I simply adore the library. It is full of books and tapes and pictures and neat displays. Our librarian's name is Mr. Counts. He is funny.

As soon as we reached the library, I ran to Mr. Counts. He was busy putting some books back on a shelf. I tapped his elbow. "Hi, Mr. Counts," I said.

He turned around. "Hello, Miss Brewer," he replied.

I laughed. "Guess what. I need to learn about capybaras," I told him. "They are animals. Wild animals. That is all I know about them."

Mr. Counts showed me the section of

animal books. Some of the books were about farm animals, some were about fish, some were about birds, and some were about cats or dogs or chimps or owls. I looked until I found three books about wild animals. Then I checked for the word *capybara* in the index. One book did not have any information about my animal, so I put it back. But the next one had a page about capybaras, plus a picture, and the third had a whole chapter on capybaras.

"Guess what," I said to Ms. Colman. "Now I know what a capybara is. It is the largest rodent in the world. See? Here's a picture of one. It lives in Central America and South America. I cannot wait to make my statue, even if the capybara is not very cute."

I checked the two wild animal books out of the library.

5

Mrs. Hoffman

Here is who was absent from Ms. Colman's room on Thursday: Ricky, Natalie, Pamela, Bobby, and Leslie Morris. Guess who else was absent from Ms. Colman's room. Ms. Colman.

When Nancy and I stepped into the classroom that morning, someone was sitting at our teacher's desk.

She was . . . a substitute.

I do not like substitutes very much. Mostly, I just like Ms. Colman. But this substitute smiled when Nancy and I came through the doorway. "Hello, Karen. Hello, Nancy," she said.

"Mrs. Hoffman!" I cried.

Once, Ms. Colman got sick and she had to be absent for more than a *month*. Mrs. Hoffman took her place. At first I did not like her at all. I called her Mrs. Hoffburger and Hatey Hoffman. But then she showed us what a nice teacher she could be. I had been sorry to say good-bye to her. Now I was happy to see her again.

"How long are you — achoo — going to be here?" I asked.

"I'm — bless you — going to be here for just a day or two," replied Mrs. Hoffman. She handed me a tissue. "Ms. Colman caught the flu, but she thinks she'll be back soon."

We had a very fun day with Mrs. Hoffman. First, we had reading.

"Ms. Colman said no reading books and no workbooks today," Mrs. Hoffman told us. (Bullfrogs. I like doing workbook pages.) "She said I should read to you instead. She said you are in the middle of *The Twenty-One Balloons.*"

Hurray! I took back my "bullfrogs." Sgor-fllub. (To take something back, you have to say it backward.)

"Oh, Mrs. Hoffman!" I called. I waved my hand around. "You will love *The Twenty-One* — achoo — *Balloons.* It is the best book!"

"Bless you, Karen," said Mrs. Hoffman again.

Then she read "Chapter Seven, The Moroccan House of Marvels." I laughed a lot. And sneezed two more times.

"Bless you, bless you," said Mrs. Hoffman. She gave me another Kleenex.

Guess what. At recess, Mrs. Hoffman came outside with our class. And she *played* with us. Even though she is old, she played Mother, May I? and SPUD. She even threw a basketball through the hoop.

In the afternoon, Mrs. Hoffman said, "Now it is science time, class. Ms. Colman said you are studying wild animals."

"Yes!" I said. "And my secret animal — achoo — is the capybara."

"Bless you," said Mrs. Hoffman. "And please remember to raise your hand."

We worked on our own. First we read about our animals in the books we had checked out of the library. Then we practiced drawing pictures of our animals. After that, Mrs. Hoffman gave us clay. She let us begin our models. I was a sculptor at last.

I had a gigundoly fun time. But I felt bad for Ricky and Natalie and the other kids who were absent. I hoped they got well soon. I especially hoped they got well by next Friday.

"Okay, please clean up, class!" Mrs. Hoffman said later.

We cleaned up our messes. Then we had a surprise. Mrs. Hoffman had brought her guitar to school. We sang "The Big Rock

Candy Mountain." It is our special Mrs. Hoffman song.

The bell rang. "Achoo! Good-bye, Mrs. Hoffman!" I called. "I'm glad you were our substitute today."

"Good-bye, Karen. Thank you. And bless you."

6

The Bad Dream

"Karen?" said Mommy. "You look very tired."

"I know," I replied. I yawned. Then I sneezed.

"Bless you," said Mommy and Seth and Andrew.

"Thank you. You know what? I do not think I can finish my supper. I'm sorry. I guess I was not very hungry." I looked at my plate. I had eaten half of my vegetables and some of my salad, but only a few bites of fish. My plate was more full than empty.

"That's okay, honey," said Mommy.

"May I please be excused?" I asked. "Achoo!"

"Of course," replied Mommy.

"Bless you," said Andrew.

I went to my room. I lay down on my bed with Goosie and Tickly.

"My head feels funny," I told Goosie. (I made him nod.) "So I think I will rest for awhile."

Before I knew it, I was asleep. I fell asleep so early that I was still wearing my school clothes. But when I woke up later, I was in my nightgown. The light was off. And the covers were tucked around Goosie and me.

I sat straight up in bed. I looked at my clock. It said one-thirty. That was late. I bet even Mommy and Seth were asleep.

"What a horrible dream," I whispered to Goosie. "Do you know what I dreamed about? I dreamed I was running through the jungle. And it was full of wild animals. The animals were friendly. Except for the gigundo snakes. They were hanging from the trees, and they were not friendly. They looked very pretty — like rainbows — but they snapped at my head when I ran underneath them. . . . Boy, my room is hot."

I kicked off my covers. I lay down again, hugging Goosie. Very soon, I was freezing cold. I was so cold I rubbed my hands together to warm them. I was so cold my teeth chattered.

"Brrrr!" I said, and I pulled up the covers again.

Soon I was too hot.

Also, my head ached.

I kicked off some of my covers but not all of them. Then I lay very still. I watched the numbers on my clock change. I wished I could go to sleep. My head would probably stop hurting if I slept.

But I was not sleepy. Guess how long I lay in bed. For a whole hour. At two-thirty I sat up again. I was uncomfortable and bored. I tiptoed downstairs. In the darkness and silence my little house seemed huge.

I turned on the light in the kitchen. Mommy had bought Oreo cookies. I opened a cabinet and found them. But I did not eat any. My tummy did not want any food.

I crept into the living room and turned on another light. A newspaper was lying on a table. I tried to read it, but my eyes hurt. Also, I was not wearing my glasses. And also I was shivering again.

I crept into the rec room. I did not turn on a lamp, but I turned on the TV, which made blue TV light. I lay down on the couch. I pulled a blanket over me. (It was Rocky's blanket and covered with fur.) I watched whatever came on the TV on Channel Four. First I watched the end of some old movie. Then I watched a show called *Our Miss Brooks*. It looked even older than the movie. After that, I watched a news program.

The news was very boring.

It was so boring I fell asleep.

Fever

"Karen? Karen?"

Someone was calling my name, but I did not want to answer. I had shrunk. I was four inches tall. And I was in Candy Land. Andrew was with me. He was only three inches tall. Candy Land looked just like our game — except that the candy was real. I was eating a peppermint stick.

"Karen? You're dreaming, honey. Wake up."

Bullfrogs. I was not in Candy Land after

all. I had been asleep. Now Mommy was shaking my shoulder.

Very slowly I opened my eyes. I was lying on the couch in the rec room at the little house. The TV had been turned off. Outside, the sun was shining.

"Mommy?" I said sleepily.

"Karen, what are you doing here?"

"I couldn't sleep last night, so I came downstairs. I watched TV. Mommy, I feel *awful*. I'm hot and achy and my head hurts and my throat hurts and my nose is stuffed up."

Mommy put her hand on my forehead. "You have a fever," she said. "You probably caught the flu."

I groaned. So *this* was how Ricky had felt on Monday.

Mommy picked me up. She carried me to my room and put me in bed. (Mommy has not carried me in ages.) Then she took my temperature. "One hundred and three degrees!" she exclaimed. "No wonder you feel awful."

"Do I have to go to school?" I asked.

"Of course not," Mommy replied. "You are going to stay right here in bed for awhile. One hundred and three is a very high fever. I will give you some Tylenol."

Andrew peered into my room. "What's wrong with Karen?" he asked.

"She caught the flu," Mommy whispered. "She does not feel well."

"Is she going to stay at home today?"

"Yes."

"Do *I* have to go to school?"

"Yes."

"Oh," said Andrew.

That morning, my little-house family was very nice to me.

Mommy said, "Do you want some breakfast, Karen? I will make tea for you. I will fix you whatever you want."

"No, thank you." My tummy still was not hungry.

"Do you want me to wheel the old TV in here?" asked Seth. "You could watch TV in bed today."

"No, thank you." Now my head hurt so much that I did not want to watch TV. Even though the *I Love Lucy* hour would come on soon.

"Do you want my new coloring book, Karen?" asked Andrew. "You can have it. Really. I only colored one page in it."

"No, thank you." What I really wanted to do was sleep some more.

Being *this* sick was not fun at all.

A little later, Andrew came into my room again. "Good-bye, Karen," he said. "Seth is going to take me to school now. You can still have my coloring book if you want it."

"Thanks," I said.

"Goody-bye, honey," said Seth. "Feel better. I'll see you tonight. Mommy will be downstairs if you need her."

"Okay," I mumbled. Then I fell asleep.

8

The Stay-at-Home Day

When I woke up later in the morning, Mommy was standing by my bed.

"Hi, Mommy!" I said. "I feel much better!"

"You do? I was thinking maybe I should call the doctor."

"The doctor! No! Take my temperature first."

Mommy did. "Well, you *are* better," she said. "You still have a fever, but now it is one hundred and one. It has dropped two degrees."

"And my head does not hurt so much."

"Good. Maybe you will get over the flu quickly."

"What time is it?" I asked. The night before seemed strange and long ago. And I was not used to sleeping in the daytime.

"Almost twelve o'clock," Mommy answered. "Andrew will be home from school soon. Would you like something to eat?"

"Yes! Now my tummy is very hungry."

Mommy smiled. "Would your tummy like some chicken noodle soup? And some toast? And maybe some ginger ale?"

"Yes, yes, and yes."

"And would your eyes like the TV now?"

"Definitely!"

That day I ate lunch in bed. I slurped up those noodles while I watched *Jeopardy* and *Let's Make a Deal* and *Concentration*. Someday, maybe I will get to be on a game show. I would like to play *Concentration*. I would like to win a car. Then I would give it to Charlie so he could drive it instead of the old Junk Bucket he drives now.

Even though the game shows were fun, I grew bored. After awhile I turned off the TV. "Mommy?" I called. "Can Andrew play with me?"

Mommy would not let Andrew play with me. She was hoping he would not catch the flu. So I read. I started a new book by Roald Dahl. Mr. Dahl wrote *Charlie and the Chocolate Factory*. I simply adore his books. His new one was called *Esio Trot*. Guess what that means. It is the word *tortoise* backward. There is a good riddle in *Esio Trot*. I finished the story that afternoon. (I read the funniest parts aloud to Goosie so he could enjoy the book, too.)

Then I yelled to Andrew to ask Mommy to bring me a soda.

Then I yelled to Andrew to ask Mommy to bring me my crayons.

And then I yelled to Andrew to ask Mommy to bring me some Tylenol.

"What's wrong, sweetie?" said Mommy when she came into my room with the children's Tylenol and a glass of juice. "Do you feel bad again?"

I nodded. "I'm all achy. And I'm hot again."

Mommy took my temperature. It had gone up. "That sometimes happens late in the afternoon," she said. "Why don't you take a nap?"

"I'm not sleepy," I said. But I took a nap anyway.

When I woke up, Seth had come home from work. Mommy was getting ready to take Andrew to Daddy's for the weekend.

"Feeling better?" Mommy asked me.

"A little," I said. "I wish I could go to Daddy's, too."

"I know you do," said Mommy. "But you don't want to give everyone the flu, do you? Anyway, you can stay here and rest. We will have a quiet weekend. Maybe you can go back to school on Monday."

"I hope so," I replied. I *had* to get better. I did not want to miss the zoo trip.

9

The Horrible,
Rotten Weekend

I slept very late on Saturday morning. Even though I had slept most of Friday morning, napped Friday afternoon, and gone to bed early Friday night. I was a lazybones.

"You are not a lazybones," Mommy said when she gave me breakfast. "You are sleeping because you are sick. Sleeping is your body's way of helping you to get better. You need your rest."

"I wish I didn't. I wish I could go to the big house."

"Not this weekend," said Mommy.

"No fair," I complained. "Andrew is there. This is a horrible, rotten weekend."

"Sorry, sweetie," said Mommy. "But look at this. I bought you an activity book." Mommy left me with the new book and a pencil and some crayons.

I opened the book. I connected a dot picture. Then I worked a crossword puzzle. After that, I looked at my watch. If I were at Daddy's, I said to myself, I would probably be playing with Hannie now. Or maybe I would be helping David Michael feed Shannon. Boo, boo, boo. I was bored.

Seth took care of that. He came into my room and read me a chapter from a very wonderful book called *Caddie Woodlawn*. The book was so wonderful that when Seth left, I read another chapter to myself. Then I realized I was hungry. "Hey, Mommy!" I yelled.

Mommy came into my room. She said she would fix me a sandwich. She would bring it to me on a tray.

"Do I *have* to stay in bed?" I whined.

"You do today," Mommy answered. "But if your temperature stays down, you may get out of bed tomorrow."

"Hurray!" I cried.

After lunch I said, "I have a good idea, Mommy. I am going to build a special invention. I will build it right here in bed. You will like it. I promise."

"Okay," said Mommy. "Make sure you stay in bed, though."

"I will. Can you bring me some string, please?"

I was going to invent a bell ringer. The bell would be a nice way to call Mommy. It would be much nicer than yelling, "Hey, Mommy!"

I wound the string around my bed. I tied one end to a handbell. This is how my invention was supposed to work: The string would make all these funny things happen, and then the bell would ring. I saw that on TV. But when I pulled the end of my string, nothing happened. I decided that ringing the bell with my hand would be just as easy.

Guess what. On Saturday afternoon my temperature did not go up. On Sunday it was normal. Mommy let me get out of bed. I even got dressed. I called my big-house family to see if everyone missed me.

"Hi, Kristy," I said. "I can go to school tomorrow. Did you miss me?"

Kristy said she had. So did everyone else.

Later, I called Nancy. "I am all better," I said.

"That is good," Nancy replied. "But six people were absent on Friday."

Uh-oh. Just because I was well did not mean we could go to the zoo. My classmates had to be well, too. All of them. And Ms. Colman had to be well.

"How are you feeling?" I asked Nancy.

"Fine," she said.

I phoned Hannie. "How are you feeling?" I asked her.

"Fine," she said.

I hoped we would *stay* fine.

10

The Mean, Green Bug

By Sunday evening I felt pretty happy. I could go to school the next day. Andrew was back from the big house. I had not missed anything. The weekend had been quiet. And *maybe* we would go to the zoo on Friday.

Before I went to sleep that night, I sang a song to Goosie. It went, *"Flu, flu, you make me feel blue, and I hate you, I really do, but now I am all well. So there!"* (Goosie whispered that he liked the song.)

I fell asleep quickly.

I dreamed another strange dream. I dreamed I was at school. Hannie and Nancy and I were in the cafeteria. Awful Pamela Harding was sitting at our table. She was eating chocolate pudding.

"Have some, Karen," she said. She pushed another container of pudding toward me. I ate the pudding. Pamela gave me more. I ate that, too. Then she gave me even *more.*

"I cannot eat that," I said. "I feel sick."

When I woke up from the dream, I really did feel sick. My tummy felt awful. Like I was on a roller coaster, but not having fun.

"Oh, no!" I cried. I sat up fast. "Mommeeeee!" I called. I ran into the bathroom. Mommy ran in after me.

"What's wrong?" she asked.

"I have to throw up," I said. And then it happened.

I *hate* throwing up. It is disgusting. I started to cry.

"Poor Karen," said Mommy.

"I have to throw up *again*," I told her.

I threw up lots of times that night. So many times that Mommy brought a pillow and a blanket into the bathroom for me. I could not leave the bathroom. And my fever came back.

Mommy took my temperature. "Only one hundred this time," she said. "Not as high as before, but it is still a fever. I guess the flu did not go away after all, honey. Sometimes that happens."

"No school tomorrow?" I asked.

"No school tomorrow," said Mommy. "You have the mean, green bug."

"Yuck."

When I woke up on Monday morning I felt much better, though. Mommy took my temperature again. "Almost normal," she said.

"Can I go to school tomorrow?"

"We'll see. It will depend on how you do today."

"Okay."

What if I was still sick on Friday, and everybody but me got to go to the zoo? That would be gigundoly awful. I *had* to get better.

So on Monday, I did everything Mommy told me to do.

In the morning I stayed quietly in bed. I did not fool around trying to invent bell ringers. Instead, I read another chapter in *Caddie Woodlawn*. Then I wrote a letter to my grandparents in the state of Nebraska. I told them I had the mean, green bug, but I was getting better.

Mommy let me eat soup and crackers for lunch. Everything stayed in my tummy, where it was supposed to stay. Mommy took my temperature. Normal. I did not have to stay in bed anymore. I ate dinner with my family. My tummy felt fine. My temperature stayed normal.

"You may go to school tomorrow," Mommy told me.

Hurray!

11

I'm Back!

When I woke up on Tuesday, Mommy said, "I better take your temperature again. Just to make sure."

It was still normal. And I felt fine. I could not wait to see my friends again. And Ms. Colman. And Hootie, our class guinea pig. And my desk. And my cubby. And the cafeteria. I felt as though I had been absent for ages.

When I got to school I rushed to my classroom.

Ricky was there! So were Natalie and Pamela. They had gotten well.

Soon Ms. Colman came into the room. I ran to her and cried, "I'm back!"

"I am so glad," replied Ms. Colman. "But please remember your indoor voice."

"Sorry," I said. "And you are back, too, Ms. Colman. Are you better?"

"I feel fine."

"So do I," I said.

I sat at my desk. I waited for the rest of the class to arrive. But *eight* kids were still missing when Ms. Colman began to take attendance.

Half the class was absent again. It was *Tues*day. We were never going to be able to go to the zoo in three days. Were we?

I asked Ms. Colman about the trip. "We will have to wait and see, Karen," she told me. "We will have to wait until Friday."

Bullfrogs.

"Today," said Ms. Colman, "we are not going to do the things we usually do. Too many students are absent. I would have to teach the lessons all over again, some other time. So instead, we are going to hold a spelling bee. And later you may work on your animal sculptures. Don't forget that you have music class today. And gym — but not for those of you who have just been sick.''

What a great day! First, the spelling bee.

I happen to be a very good speller. Once I was even the runner-up in a state spelling competition. I got to be on TV.

Each team wanted me on their side.

That day, I did not miss one word. I won the game for my team. This is the word I won with: cafeteria. Isn't that long? Nine letters.

In music class we learned how to sing "Do Re Mi." Then we sang it in a round, which was fun until Natalie got confused. She sang the wrong verse. Then everyone else got confused, too.

I could not take gym that day, since I had been absent the day before. That is the rule.

I like gym. But Ms. Colman let me and the other kids who had been sick go to the library. And in the library was a storyteller. He told the story of Peter and the Wolf. He used lots of sound effects.

In the afternoon, we worked on our animal sculptures. My capybara needed lots of work. Some of the other sculptures looked almost finished. But I was not sure what most of them were. I did not see an elephant or a bear or a tiger or a lion. Just weird animals.

"What's yours?" I asked Ricky. "It looks like a monkey."

"It is a marmoset," he told me. "And it *is* a kind of monkey. They live in trees. In South America. Mostly they eat insects. Guess what the smallest kind of marmoset is called."

"I give up," I told Ricky.

"A pygmy marmoset. Pygmy marmosets only get to be *six inches* long, not counting their tails."

"Gosh," I said. "That is very tiny." I

went back to work on my capybara. I was shaping his feet. I wanted the feet to look just right. Then I changed my mind. I crossed two of the capybara's toes. This was for good luck. For the zoo trip on Friday.

12

The Great Animal Fact Hunt

The next day was Wednesday. I went to school with my fingers crossed. Nancy was with me. I made her cross her fingers, too.

Bad news. *Eight* kids were absent again. Only they were not the same eight kids who had been absent on Tuesday. Two of those kids had gotten well. They were back in school. Two other kids had just gotten sick. They were absent for the first time. Those kids were Jannie and . . . Hannie. Oh, no! Hannie *had* to get better fast. She and Nancy and I were going to stick together on the zoo trip. Best friends always stick together.

That afternoon we worked on our sculptures again. My capybara was almost finished. I even began to paint him. (I named him Prince Charming.)

On Thursday I went to school with my fingers crossed. Also, I held my breath. My magic must have worked because only three kids were absent. And Hannie was back! She looked fine.

"I just had a little cold," she told Nancy and me. "Not the flu."

When Ms. Colman took attendance that morning, I waved my hand in the air. "Oh, Ms. Colman, Ms. Colman!" I cried. "Only three people are absent today. If three people are absent tomorrow, will we go on our trip?"

"Karen, let's wait until tomorrow," said my teacher. "We will see how many people are absent. Until then, think positively."

"Okay," I replied. I thought, We *will* go to the zoo. We *will* go to the zoo. We *will* go to the zoo.

Ms. Colman must have been thinking positively, too. She acted as if we would be going on our trip the next day. First she gave us some reminders: "You can buy lunch at the zoo cafeteria, but you might want to bring a soda or a drink with you. Also, if you have not yet given me your permission slip, please bring it to school tomorrow. And remember the bus rules. You must stay in your seats. And you must sit with your partner."

"What partner?" asked Ricky.

Ms. Colman smiled. "I was just going to tell you about that. I want each of you to choose someone who will be your partner on the trip. You must stay with your partner all day."

"Can we choose anyone for our partner?" I asked.

"Yes."

"Can we choose two partners?"

"No."

Bullfrogs. Of course, I wanted both Hannie and Nancy to be my partners. We wanted to stick together. But we could not do that. Finally, I decided to be Nancy's partner, and Hannie decided to be Natalie's partner. We would stay together as much as we could.

When we had chosen partners, Ms. Colman said, "While you are at the zoo, you will work on a project. You will go on The Great Animal Fact Hunt."

Cool! I thought.

"You will divide into three groups of partners," Ms. Colman went on. "Each group will complete a worksheet. The worksheets will be different. You will need to find animal facts at the zoo. A room mother or room father will be with you to help you and to be your group leader."

"Is the fact hunt a contest?" I asked.

"No. But if your group fills out your sheet

correctly, every member of your group will receive a small prize."

Oh, please, oh, please, oh, please — we have to go to the zoo tomorrow! I thought.

That afternoon, I worked very hard on Prince Charming, and I finished him.

13

Off to the Zoo

Here is how many people were absent on Friday, zoo day: one. Jannie was the only kid who could not come to school.

"We will go to the zoo," announced Ms. Colman.

I almost shouted, "Yea! Hurray!" But I did not. This is why. The three room parents were standing near Ms. Colman's desk. Guess who one of the fathers was. Daddy! He was coming to the zoo with us. I promised myself to stay on my very best behavior that day. I did not want him to hear anyone remind me to use my indoor voice.

That morning, Ms. Colman did not make us sit at our desks. She said we could sit anywhere we wanted. Natalie, Hannie, Nancy, and I sat on some desks in the back of the room.

"Look at this," said Hannie, jumping off the desk. She pulled a wallet out of her pocket. "Here is how much money I brought with me. I have been saving my allowance. I bet I could buy a really good souvenir with this."

Ms. Colman had told us about the souvenir shop at the zoo. She had said we might have time to visit it. I hoped we would. I like to buy souvenirs.

Natalie held out a paper bag. "Look what kind of soda I brought," she said. "It is called Fresca and it is so, so delicious."

"Mommy made me bring juice," I said. "Apple juice."

"*My* mother made me bring milk," said Nancy.

60

"Mine, too," said Hannie.

"Class?" Ms. Colman called from the front of the room. "May I have your attention, please? Listen up. I want to talk about what to do if you get lost from your group. Who remembers?"

Nancy's hand shot up. "I do," she said. "We should look around for an adult. A grown-up. Especially someone who works at the zoo."

"Right," agreed Ms. Colman. "Should you look very far?"

Bobby Gianelli raised his hand. "No. We should try to stay in one place, because we will be easier to find."

"Great," said our teacher. "What else?"

"Listen for announcements," I answered. "And follow instructions."

"Perfect!" exclaimed Ms. Colman. (Daddy smiled at me.) "All right. Please make sure you have your drinks with you. It is time to get on the bus to the zoo."

I could not help myself. I let out one tiny "Hurray!"

The Wheels on the Bus

"Please find your partners," said Ms. Colman. "And hold hands."

"Hold hands!" cried Bobby. "No way! I'm not holding Ricky's hand."

Ms. Colman just said, "Please hold hands until you get on the bus."

I took Nancy's hand. (Bobby held onto the sleeve of Ricky's coat.) Then we walked out of our room in our double line of partners. We walked down the hall and across the parking lot. A yellow school bus was waiting for us. We climbed up the steps.

Nancy and I sat in the very back seat. Hannie and Natalie sat right in front of us.

"We are going to the zoo!" I cried. "We are going on a fact hunt!"

Everyone else was as excited as I was. Except maybe for the adults. They sat together at the front of the bus. They did not shout.

Soon the driver pulled the bus away from school. We drove through town. My friends and I talked and laughed. The driver flew over a little bump in the road — and the people in the back bounced into the air.

"Do that again!" I called.

Across the aisle sat Ricky and Bobby. In front of them were Pamela and Leslie. Leslie's braids hung over the back of the seat. Bobby was busily trying to poke a paper clip through the end of one.

We drove out of Stoneybrook. We turned onto a highway.

Just then Natalie said, "Uh-oh."

"What?" asked Hannie.

"I am bus sick. My stomach does not like being bumped up and down."

"Are you going to barf?" I asked.

"Maybe," said Natalie.

"Ms. Colman!" I shrieked. "Daddy! Natalie is going to barf!"

Ms. Colman hurried to the back of the bus.

"I only said I *might* barf," Natalie told our teacher. "I am getting bus sick. I need to sit up front."

So Natalie and Hannie had to switch places with Audrey and Sara. One of the room mothers gave Natalie a plastic bag to barf in. Luckily, Natalie did not need to use it. She held it in her lap, though.

"Let's sing songs!" called Leslie. (She was wearing a paper clip in one of her braids, but she did not know it.)

"Good idea," said Ms. Colman. "I know the perfect song for a field trip. How about 'The Wheels on the Bus'?"

"Yea!" I cried.

My classmates and I sang, *"The wheels on*

the bus go round and round, round and round, round and round. The wheels on the bus go round and round, all about the town."

Then we sang some other verses: *"The driver of the bus says, 'Move on back!' "* and, *"The wipers on the bus go back and forth,"* and, *"The people on the bus go bump, bump, bump."*

"I have a new verse!" Pamela Harding announced. She sang, *"The people in the back bounce up, up, up!"*

And Ricky said, "I have a new verse, too." He sang, *"Natalie Springer goes barf, barf, barf, barf, barf, barf, barf, barf, barf. Natalie Springer goes barf, barf, barf, all across the floor!"*

"I did not barf!" Natalie shouted.

"Class, please settle down," called Ms. Colman.

So we did. Until we saw a sign that said TO THE ZOO.

The Kinkajou

I almost jumped out of my seat and shouted, "We're here!" Then I remembered Daddy was sitting in the front of the bus. So I just turned to Nancy and whispered, "We're here. We are at the zoo!"

"Please file off of the bus," said Ms. Colman. "And stay with your partners."

Nancy and I stood in the parking lot, holding hands. We looked around us.

"I see a giraffe's head," said Nancy.

"I see the top of the . . . the bird cage. What is it called?"

"The aviary?" said Nancy.

"Yeah, the aviary. Oh, boy. This is going to be awesome!"

"Class, please follow me," said Ms. Colman. She led us through a gate and into the zoo. One of the room mothers collected the drinks we had brought for lunch. She took them to the cafeteria.

While she was gone, Ms. Colman divided us into our three groups. Guess who was in charge of my group. Daddy. He was going to be our leader. Yea! The kids in my group were Nancy, me, Hannie, Natalie, Ricky, and Bobby.

"Do you remember your zoo manners?" Ms. Colman asked my class.

"Yes!" we answered.

"Do you remember what to do if you cannot find your group?"

"Yes!"

"Good. Now I will show you the visitors center and the cafeteria. They are places you could go to if you need help." Ms. Colman pointed out the buildings. Finally she handed a worksheet to each group.

I looked at ours. I saw a list of sentences with blanks, like this: "The largest reptile known to man is _____. It lives in _____." And like this: "The kinkajou is a nocturnal, arboreal mammal. It lives in _____, in Central and South America. Another name for the kinkajou is _____."

"We will have to find a lot of answers," I said to Daddy. "How will we know where to look for them?"

"The sentences are clues," replied Daddy. "To fill in the first blanks, we will go to the reptile house. To find out about kinkajous, we will go to the building where the nocturnal animals live."

"Oh, I see," I said. "Cool!"

"Class?" said Ms. Colman. "Please give me your attention. Does everybody understand how the groups will work? Each worksheet is different, so the groups will go off in different directions. Please stay together and stay with your group leader.

Your leader will help you fill in the blanks. I will walk around the zoo and check on each group. Let's meet at the cafeteria at noon for lunch. Afterward, you may continue the fact hunt. Most important, have fun today! Enjoy the animals."

The fact hunt was about to begin.

My friends and I looked at our sheet again.

"Okay, let's go to the reptile house first," said Daddy.

"Excuse me, sir," spoke up Natalie. "Is a snake a reptile?"

"Yes," Daddy answered.

"Then I do not think I want to go in the reptile house."

That was how our fact hunt began. Daddy stood in the doorway of the reptile house where he could watch Natalie (outside) and the rest of us (inside). We filled in the first sentences on our sheet. The largest reptile known to man is *the saltwater crocodile*. It lives in *Southeast Asia and other parts of the world*.

16

Karen's Alligator

My friends and Daddy and I walked all around the zoo. Do you want to know what the kinkajou lives in? It lives in trees. Only trees. That is what *arboreal* means. Can you imagine never touching the ground? And the other name for a kinkajou is honey bear.

"Honey bear," I said as I read the sign in front of the kinkajou's cage. "I like that name. I think I will change my teddy's name. I will call him Honey Bear from now on."

We looked at the animals of Africa and

the monkeys in the ape house and the birds in the aviary. When we left the aviary, Daddy said, "Kids? It is almost twelve o'clock. It is time to go to the cafeteria."

We were the last ones to reach the cafeteria! The kids in my class, plus the group leaders, plus Ms. Colman were already there. Hannie and Nancy and Natalie and I each got a tray. We walked through the food line. Here is what I bought: a peanut butter sandwich, an apple, a brownie, and then another brownie. I had never seen so many choices. That cafeteria served lasagna and hamburgers and lots of kinds of sandwiches and vegetables and salads and cake and cookies and doughnuts. . . . Yum!

Hannie and Nancy and Natalie and I ate at a little round table. Daddy brought our drinks to us. We pretended we were eating in a fancy restaurant and Daddy was our waiter. His name was Garçon.

After lunch, Ms. Colman made a very wonderful announcement. "Before you start the fact hunt again," she said, "you

may go to the souvenir shop. You have time to buy one souvenir each."

"*Yes!*" I whispered to Nancy. "The souvenir shop! All *right!*"

The souvenir shop was next door to the cafeteria. It was very big. And it was full of cool stuff. Hannie and Nancy and I hardly knew where to look first. Finally we all looked at different things. Hannie looked through a rack of zoo T-shirts. Nancy looked at some books about animals. I looked at the animal toys. I saw animal erasers. I saw glow-in-the-dark dinosaurs. I saw rubber snakes and spiders. And then I saw . . . biting alligators. At one end of a yellow stick was an alligator head. At the other end was a handle. When I squeezed the handle, the alligator's mouth opened and closed.

That was the souvenir for me.

"Hey, Hannie!" I called.

Hannie was holding up a T-shirt. "What?" she said.

I stuck out the alligator. I made it nip at Hannie's nose. "Gotcha!" I said.

Hannie giggled. "Let me try," she said. Hannie made the alligator bite Nancy. Nancy made the alligator bite me again. And I made the alligator bite Ricky and Natalie and Bobby.

"Gotcha, gotcha, gotcha!" I cried.

"Karen," said Daddy. "Please settle down."

Uh-oh. "Sorry," I said.

When we had paid for our souvenirs, Ms. Colman collected them. "I will put them on the bus," she said. "They will be waiting for you when we leave the zoo." Then she went on, "Class, it is time to continue the fact hunt. You have until one-thirty to finish your worksheets. At one-thirty, we will meet at the seal pool. Good luck!"

Daddy and my friends and I looked at our worksheet. Then we set off again. This time we were headed for the exhibit of desert animals.

17

The Sea Lion

My group and I walked all over the zoo. We were very busy. We saw eagles and elephants and cougars and turtles and hyenas. I never knew there were so many different animals. If I made a list of the animals I saw at the zoo, I bet it would be as long as the school bus.

Even though I was having fun, I began to feel sad.

"Daddy," I said, "I do not like to see

animals in cages. I feel sorry for them. You know what? We are supposed to be learning about wild animals. But *these* animals are not wild. The zoo people take care of them and feed them. Plus, the animals do not have any privacy. They live in cages, and every day people stare at them and point at them."

Daddy took my hand. "You are right, Karen," he said. "Visiting the zoo is fun. And it is a good way to learn about animals. And maybe some animals *like* being around lots of people. But I am sure that some do not like it. I feel sorry about those animals, too."

I did not feel sad for very long, though. That is because we finally finished our worksheet. Our fact hunt was over.

"What time is it?" I asked Daddy.

"Time to go to the seal pool," he answered. "It is almost one-thirty. You worked hard today, kids. You did a good job."

Nancy and Hannie and Natalie and Ricky and Bobby and I let out a cheer. Then we ran alongside Daddy, all the way to the seal pool.

We had been to the seal pool earlier that afternoon. We had filled in some sentences on our worksheet. The sentences were about sea lions. They are a kind of seal. They like to eat fish. Most boy lions have *manes!*

"Hello, everybody!" I called when my group reached the seal pool. The rest of my class was already there. So were the group leaders. Ms. Colman was not there, but we were a little early. It was not quite one-thirty.

Hannie and Nancy and I looked at our worksheet. We read over our answers again.

"They must be right," I said.

"Yeah, we worked hard on them," added Nancy.

"We were very careful," said Hannie.

"I wonder what our prizes will be," I said.

"Hey!" cried Hannie. "Maybe they will be free trips to the zoo!"

"Oh, that would be gigundoly wonderful!" I exclaimed.

Ms. Colman Is Missing

My class and I waited and waited. We talked a lot about the prizes.

Bobby hoped we would each win a biting alligator so we could have a biting-alligator contest on the way home.

"But I already *have* a biting alligator," I complained.

Natalie hoped we would win a new pet for our classroom. She said if she could choose any pet at all it would be a pink flamingo.

"Daddy, what time is it?" I asked.

"One forty," he answered. "Twenty minutes until two o'clock."

Hmm. Ms. Colman was ten minutes late. She is not usually late.

I leaned over the railing around the seal pool. I watched the sea lions. I liked their gentle, dark eyes.

"*Now* what time is it?" I asked Daddy.

He sighed. "It is one forty-five."

Five minutes later he said, "Now it is one fifty. Ten minutes until two."

"Daddy, Ms. Colman is twenty minutes late!" I cried. "Something has happened!"

"Oh, Karen," said Daddy, but I interrupted him.

"Ms. Colman is missing!" I exclaimed.

"Maybe she got lost," Hannie suggested.

"We know what to do if someone gets lost," said Ricky proudly.

"Yeah, exactly what to do," agreed Natalie. "Go find the lost person. Tell him to wait right where he is. Then say the person's name over the loudspeaker and ask him to meet you in the cafeteria."

Well, for heaven's sake. "Natalie," I said, "if you have already found the lost person, then you do not have to call him and tell him where to meet you."

"Oh," said Natalie.

"But, Daddy, Natalie is sort of right," I said. "We should ask someone to say Ms. Colman's name over the loudspeaker. And to tell her to come find us at the seal pool, because we are waiting for her. If one of *us* was lost, *Ms. Colman* would say that person's name over the loudspeaker."

"I suppose so," said Daddy. "But, honey, Ms. Colman is a grown-up. She knows we are waiting for her at the seal pool. And she knows how to find the seal pool. She will ask for directions if she needs to."

"Daddy, *please*."

"Karen, I do not think it is necessary."

I burst into tears. "Our teacher is lost and you do not even care," I cried.

"I *do* care — " Daddy began to say.

At the same time, another voice said,

"Goodness, I am late! I'm *very* sorry. I did not mean to be late. Thank you for waiting so patiently."

My teacher was back!

"Oh, Ms. Colman. I thought you were missing!" I exclaimed. "I thought you were lost. We almost called your name on the loudspeaker. Hey, guess what. All the groups finished their worksheets. If we found the right answers, what prizes do we get?" I hopped from one foot to the other.

"Calm down, please," Ms. Colman said gently. "I will tell you about the prizes in a little while. First, I have a surprise."

"For *me?*" I squeaked.

"Well, for everyone. Please follow me to the visitors center now."

The three groups and the three parents followed Ms. Colman through the zoo to the visitors center.

"A prize and a *sur*prise!" I whispered excitedly to Nancy. "I wonder what they will be. Oh, this is the best, best zoo trip of my life!"

"We're Famous!"

My friends and I waited in the hallway of the visitors center. When everyone had arrived, Ms. Colman said, "Class, I would like you to see the new display here at the zoo. You will be the first class to see it. I think you will be interested in it. And I know you will be surprised."

"A new display," whispered Bobby. He sounded disappointed. "Bor-ing."

"Yeah, bor-ing," echoed Ricky. "I bet it

will be a bunch of pictures of the guy who started the zoo or something."

"Come on, you guys," I said. "If Ms. Colman said we will be surprised, then we will be surprised."

"We will be surprised at how bored we are," said Bobby.

But he was wrong.

Ms. Colman led my class down a hallway. At the end of the hallway was a fancy room with a high ceiling.

"This room," said Ms. Colman, "is where groups gather before they go on guided zoo tours. Lots of people come to the room. While they wait for their tour to begin, they look at the displays."

"So?" I heard Bobby whisper to Ricky. (Ricky shrugged his shoulders.)

Ms. Colman stepped over to a big glass display case. "And this is the display visitors will see this month."

My class followed Ms. Colman. I was the first person to reach the case. I read the sign next to the case: *Wild Animal Sculptures by Ms. Colman's Second-Grade Class at Stoneybrook Academy.*

"Hey! Hey!" I cried. (It was hard to be excited and still use my indoor voice, but I managed.) "That's us! I mean, those are our sculptures! Look! There's mine!" Sure enough, sitting on a shelf in the case was Prince Charming. In front of him was a label: *Capybara, by Karen Brewer.* Next to Prince Charming was a fierce-looking cat. The label in front of the cat read: *Snow leopard, by Hannie Papadakis.*

I nudged Hannie. "Our animals are together!" I exclaimed softly.

Suddenly all of my classmates were crowding around the display. They were asking Ms. Colman questions like, "How did our statues get here?"

"While I was arranging the trip," said my teacher, "I told the woman who runs the visitors center about your sculptures. She wanted to display them. So yesterday afternoon, I brought them to the zoo."

"You know," I said to Nancy and Hannie, "I do not remember seeing our animals in school this morning. But I was too excited to care."

"They were here at the zoo," murmured Nancy.

"Yeah, where everyone will see them," I added. "We're famous!"

We looked and looked at the display. We counted the animals. We read our names. After awhile Ms. Colman said, "Class, I have looked over your worksheets."

Already? I thought. Oh, boy!

"I can tell you worked very hard. And I am happy to say that every answer on each worksheet is correct. So I have prizes for all of you."

"Yea," I whispered to Nancy, remembering my indoor voice.

Ms. Colman handed each of us a patch. The patch was decorated with a picture of a tiger, and the words *Bedford Zoo*.

"You may sew your patch onto your

jeans or your jacket or a book bag," said Ms. Colman. "Then you will think of our trip every time you see the patch."

I raised my hand. "Ms. Colman?" I said. "Thank you."

The Best Trip Ever

When we left the visitors center it was time to go home. It was time to go back to Stoneybrook.

My friends and I and Ms. Colman and the room parents climbed onto our bus again. The first thing I did was call out, "Hey, Ms. Colman! Where are our souvenirs? I need my alligator."

"Be patient, Karen," said my teacher. "When everyone is sitting down, I will give back the souvenirs."

And she did. Soon the bus was pulling out of the parking lot. I turned to Nancy and smiled. We were sitting in the backseat again. But Hannie and Natalie were sitting all the way up in the front of the bus, near Daddy. Hannie said she did not want to take a chance on Natalie barfing, since Natalie had eaten *three* desserts in the cafeteria. But Hannie should not have bothered worrying. Why? Because Natalie fell asleep and slept all the way home. She slept with her mouth open. She snored a little bit.

"Let's sing," said Ricky suddenly. And he sang, *"The wheels on the bus go round and round, round and round, round and round. The wheels on the bus go round and round, all about the town. . . . Natalie Springer goes snore, snore, snore"* (only he did not *say* "snore"; he just made a snoring sound effect), *"snore, snore, snore, snore, snore, snore. Natalie Springer goes snore, snore, snore, all about the town."*

The song woke Natalie. "I DO NOT SNORE!" she yelled.

"Indoor voice, Natalie," said Ms. Colman.

All *right!* I thought. Finally, Ms. Colman had told someone to use her indoor voice — and it was not me.

My classmates and I settled down again. Natalie went back to sleep. I began to feel sort of sleepy myself. For awhile, nobody talked. Ms. Colman walked up and down the aisle, checking on us.

"Ms. Colman, did you buy a souvenir?" I whispered. Ms. Colman nodded. "You did? What did you buy?" I asked.

Ms. Colman opened her purse. She pulled out a booklet. She handed it to me. It was a collection of postcards. Each one showed an animal at the zoo.

"The postcards are for Jannie," said Ms. Colman. "Because she missed the trip."

"That's nice," I said. And I meant it, even though I do not like Jannie very much. I felt bad that she had not been able to come to the Bedford Zoo.

Ms. Colman went back to her seat. I played with my alligator. I made it bite Nancy's coat. But Nancy was asleep, so that was no fun. Then I looked at my prize, the zoo patch. I decided I would ask Mommy or Seth to sew it to the cuff of my jean jacket.

After awhile, I fell asleep myself. When I woke up, we were riding through downtown Stoneybrook. We were almost back at school. Everyone else was waking up, too. Our trip was nearly over.

"Today was gigundoly fun," I said to Nancy.

"Gigundoly," she agreed.

"I will always remember it."

"Me, too."

"Hey, can you come over and play tomorrow? It will be a little-house weekend. We could play zoo. You could be a zookeeper, and I could be every single animal."

"Okay," replied Nancy.

The bus pulled up in front of Stoney-

brook Academy. My friends and I walked slowly off the bus.

"Good-bye, Ms. Colman," I said. "See you on Monday. And thank you for the best school trip ever. I will always remember our day at the zoo."

About the Author

ANN M. MARTIN lives in New York City and loves animals, especially cats. She has two cats of her own, Mouse and Rosie.

Other books by Ann M. Martin that you might enjoy are *Stage Fright*; *Me and Katie (the Pest)*; and the books in *The Baby-sitters Club* series.

Ann likes ice cream and *I Love Lucy*. And she has her own little sister, whose name is Jane.

THE BABY-SITTERS CLUB

Don't miss #25

KAREN'S PEN PAL

"Bobby," called Ms. Colman. She handed him an envelope. "Natalie." Ms. Colman handed her an envelope, too.

I sat at my desk. I sat quietly, even though my stomach was jumping around. Ms. Colman was handing out letters from our pen pals! Miss Mandel had sent them to her. I was waiting to hear my teacher call out, "Karen!" Then she would give me a letter from Maxie.

"Karen!" said Ms. Colman.

"Yes! Yes!" I reached for the envelope Ms. Colman held out. It looked quite fat. I wondered what was in it besides a letter.

LITTLE APPLE®

BABY-SITTERS

Little Sister™

by Ann M. Martin, author of *The Baby-sitters Club*®

More Titles... ➡